COYOTE AND RABBIT

A Tale from the Southwest

by Roy Lewis
illustrated by Cathy Shimmen

HOUGHTON MIFFLIN HARCOURT
School Publishers

Copyright © by Houghton Mifflin Harcourt Publishing Company

Printed in China

ISBN-10: 0-547-25288-9
ISBN-13: 978-0-547-25288-9

6 7 8 0940 18 17 16 15 14 13 12
4500350925

Coyote always had trouble with Rabbit. Coyote was swift, but Rabbit seemed just a bit swifter. Coyote was clever, but Rabbit was more clever.

The two animals would never live near each other peacefully. Coyote said to himself, "I will teach Rabbit a lesson."

The next morning, Coyote heard Hawk
and Crow.

"What a big storm last night!" said Crow.

"Yes! Lightning hit a tree and started a fire.
It blazed up over the canyon. Then it hit a big
rock on the canyon rim," Hawk said. "The rock
fell into the canyon. You know the opening at
the end?"

"Where the stream flows when there is a big rain?" asked Crow.

"Yes, that's the place. It is blocked now and the stream is empty," said Hawk. "The rock fell to the bottom, so the opening is closed. So there is only one way out for those without wings."

Coyote was very excited about what he had heard. He had once chased Rabbit up that canyon; but then Rabbit had made a leap sideways, and he had gone through a hole too small for Coyote to get through. Now Coyote could try this again. This time the small hole would be gone.

The next day, Coyote flung himself in front of Rabbit as he hopped into the canyon. "Rabbit thinks he will fool me. This time he will be the fool," Coyote said to himself.

Coyote's plan worked. When Rabbit ran into the canyon, he did not know the way was blocked. He came to the place where he had leaped sideways before. Now there was no way out.

Rabbit looked this way and that. He saw that there was no longer an escape. Still he sat calmly. "I must praise you, Coyote, because it seems you have been smarter than I," said Rabbit.

Coyote liked to hear this. He liked to think he was wise.

"I have an offer for you," said Rabbit. "It is true that you planned well. Yet it was not you who put this rock into my path."

Coyote knew it was true.

"I would like to make you an offer you would be foolish to refuse. If you let me go today, I will teach you our tricks. Then you can catch rabbits whenever you want."

"Why should I let you go?" said Coyote.

"Well, you can feed yourself today, or you can learn how to eat well every day," said Rabbit.

"You will trick me and run away," said Coyote.

"No, I will not," Rabbit said. "I will show you how we trick you and get away."

"How can I trust someone who has fooled me so many times?" asked Coyote.

"Rabbit always keeps his word," said Rabbit.

"Okay," said Coyote. "Teach me what I must know."

Rabbit showed Coyote how he could get tangled in some bushes to hide. But Coyote already knew this. Rabbit showed Coyote how he often ran in circles. But Coyote knew this, too. Rabbit showed him how he stopped so quickly that Coyote would just run right past him.

"I have seen these things many times. So show me a trick I don't know," said Coyote.

"My best trick is a quick step to the side," said Rabbit. "Try it."

Coyote tried it many times.
But he could not do it like Rabbit.

"Your eyes are in the wrong place," said Rabbit.

"There's nothing wrong with my eyes," said Coyote.

"Not for a Coyote," said Rabbit. "I am a rabbit, so my eyes are on the sides of my head. I see well to the side. Your eyes are in the front of your head. You cannot see to the side."

"Try turning your head to the side and keeping it there," said Rabbit. "Then you will be able to see to jump to the side."

"It's not very easy," said Coyote.

"Let's practice it a few times," said Rabbit.

Coyote turned his head and tried jumping to the side many times slowly.

"There's not a lot of space to practice here. Let's get out of the canyon," said Rabbit. They climbed out of the canyon and onto the rim.

Coyote and Rabbit practiced. Rabbit jumped sideways, and Coyote jumped with him. Coyote did not like holding his head to the side because he could not see where he was going. Still, he wanted to be able to catch Rabbit at any time.

"Let's try it once more," said Rabbit.

They moved along the edge of the canyon rim. Rabbit ran very fast. Coyote ran after him.

"Get ready!" yelled Rabbit. This time Rabbit did not jump sideways. He stopped. Coyote was looking to the side and did not see him. He tripped over Rabbit and fell over the edge of the canyon. Coyote was tumbling in the air!

Rabbit peeked over the edge of the canyon. Coyote was lying at the bottom. "You have tricked me again!" shouted Coyote.

"I have kept my word and showed you my tricks," said Rabbit. "There was just one more. Now you have seen it!"

"Yes, I guess I have," said Coyote.

Coyote still chases Rabbit to this day. When he does, he always holds his head to the front. You may see him move his head quickly from side to side. But he will not leave it there. He is waiting for the day when he will catch clever Rabbit.

Responding

TARGET SKILL **Cause and Effect** In this tale, Coyote tried to trick Rabbit. This caused other things to happen. Copy the chart below. Write what happened.

Cause	Effect
Coyote tried to trick Rabbit.	

Write About It

Text to World Make notes for a research report about folktales about Coyote. Include details that help readers learn about these special kinds of folktales.

✔ **TARGET SKILL** **Cause and Effect** Tell how one event makes another happen.

✔ **TARGET STRATEGY** **Visualize** Picture what is happening as you read.

GENRE A **folktale** is a story that is often told by people of a country.